THE MYSTICAL TREEHOUSE

and

OTHER FUN STORIES

"MENTORING WRITERS"
COMPETITION WINNERS 2020

All the stories in this book were written by new, developing, and established authors who entered our Summer 2020 Writing Competition. They are based on a specific selection of titles.

All entries were judged by a panel of independent judges who each gave their opinion and a score on each story. We have only included a small number from a larger selection.

We congratulate all those included in this year's book and commiserate with those who didn't quite make it.

We hope you will have better success this year.

To our readers, we hope you enjoy the stories as much as our judges did.

MENTORING WRITERS
COMPETITION 2021

If you want to enter the free 2021 Mentoring Writers Writing Competition then please email us for a copy of the submission details. There is no age limit.

contact@mentoringwriters.co.uk

www.mentoringwriters.co.uk

STORIES

THE MYSTICAL TREEHOUSE
By Shevon Claire

Overall Competition Winner

The tree in the back corner of the yard looked different? It was a Red Gum (a eucalyptus tree with redwood) and had dividing branches at a point where her head customarily reached. Today, Kerry headed for what looked like an elevator to the right of the massive trunk. Stepping up onto the platform, she pulled herself up, using the pulley system. She had hardly started when she felt her small dog join her, and after ascending only a meter higher, felt her cat landing accurately on her shoulders.

From her position in the box-shaped form, Kerry peered down onto the overgrown lawn and weeds, now shrouded in a white mist. It all looked more like part of her dreams. She seemed to have entered a kind of magical zone, where the reality of her life no longer existed. She stepped off the platform into a space that she'd never seen before. It was confusing; she was sure she heard the sound of stringed instruments.

All at once, an apparition stood in front of her. It was a woman, ethereal in appearance, with a serene expression on her face which made Kerry want to bow at her feet. What did all this mean? Had she spent too much time reading fantasy stories, so she now associated them with her real life?

Kerry felt herself rising from the floor of the treehouse; where was she going? The vision gently took her hand; a warmth emanated from the area where they touched.

"Come, Kerry, we will visit with Aaron for a little while, and then you can return to your parents," said the vision.

"Who is Aaron? Who are you?" Kerry wasn't sure if she had spoken out loud.

"It's alright, Kerry, you can call me Celeste. Aaron is going to be your little brother. He will not join you for another year, but when he does, you will guide him," Celeste told her.

"How do you know this. My mother has been very sick, and she is aware it is not likely she can have more children. Father is annoyed as he wants a little boy."

"Yes, we know that, which is why we are working to make sure that Aaron can come and live with you, very soon. He'll need all your love, and understanding more than anything else. Your parents will both love him and feel despair over him. But, it will all be worth it in the end for it will be you who helps them overcome despair. You who will love them all equally."

Suddenly Celeste came to a halt. Kerry looked to where she was indicating.

There was a baby, with tufts of blonde hair, blowing bubbles from his mouth. He was laughing.

Then the vision was replaced, with one of a little boy aged about three. He was running, falling, getting up, then running again. As she watched the changes taking place, Kerry became absorbed with the joy and excitement that Aaron exhibited. He had the freedom to choose everything around him.

Her gaze shifted to Celeste. "What is it you want me to see, there is nothing in these visions that would cause despair," Kerry whispered, still absorbed in the images of the little boy.

"Aaron will be born blind. He will need his big sister to interpret the world around him until he is confident enough to negotiate on his own," Celeste told her gently.

All at once, Kerry pointed out. "He's running, laughing, and happy. But, if he continues into the open space, he'll end up in the water. He won't be safe, and he could drown."

"That's why you need to ask your father to build a treehouse, just like this one, so when Aaron explores, you will always be able to see him."

The mist lifted a little, making Kerry take a look around.

The first thing she noted was the walls were all a uniform height. The door was a half-size one (like a stable door) but had swung shut on a spring. There was a padded seat fastened to the wall, but it could easily convert into a bed. A table sat in the middle of the room, close enough for the padded seat, but no other seating was needed.

"My father will not know how to build something like this. How am I supposed to convince him?" Kerry looked at Celeste for an answer.

"I'm confident that you will think of something; after all, the reward will be the brother you've all been praying for." And with that, Celeste disappeared.

Kerry sat looking around the treehouse, wondering if Celeste was an angel sent from God? Up until now, she wasn't sure that there was a heaven, let alone angels. Did this mean the fear she felt, that her mother was going to die, wasn't justified?

While she contemplated the situation, her father came out of the back door of the house. He looked tired and beaten as if he was ready to give up, not knowing what to do next. Seeing him helped her to make a decision. She would ask him to build her a treehouse, just like the one she'd seen.

Being careful not to fall, she clambered down the tree using the branches as hand and footholds, as the lift was no longer present. When she reached the ground, she walked up to her father, put her arms around his waist, and cuddled him.

"Dad! Can we build a treehouse?"

"Kerry, what a great idea. We can put a platform in, and you can be my apprentice and help me to build it."

"Do you think we could put in a type of lift to get us up there, with pulleys, or you know, those wheely things? That way, if I'm bringing something up into the treehouse, I'm not likely to fall like I might from a ladder." Kerry was trying her best to remember all the small details of what she'd seen while with Celeste.

"How about we go inside and start drawing it up. You can add the things that I miss from the design," her father told her as they moved towards the back door.

"When can we start building it? We need to do it in a way that doesn't damage or stress the tree. Did you know that trees can get stressed and lose all their leaves?" It was strange how Kerry kept coming up with all this information.

"So, you do listen to what I'm saying to you about climbing the tree and not causing damage, that's how you know trees get stressed. Once we've completed the drawing, I can work out what we need and then look at when we can start," replied Kerry's father.

They both went into the house, unaware of Celeste, who stood smiling and watching from the misty treehouse. She'd found a way to gain Kerry's interest, diverting her father from his anger. All she had to do now was to ensure the return to health of her mother.

Each time her father went for supplies at the local salvage yard, Kerry attended with him. Their weekends were spent first with buying supplies, and

then with beginning the construction. After each visit, they would revise the drawings, making sure that they would have everything necessary before they started.

Over the months that it took to construct the treehouse, Kerry climbed the tree many times, up the ladder her father had secured with ropes. Each time she would look for Celeste.

"Celeste, are you here?" She would ask.

Most of the time, she didn't receive a reply. But, on those days, when she was feeling without hope, Celeste would appear. Each time Kerry would ask the same question.

"Can I please see Aaron again?"

It was the image of the little boy which kept her motivated, and on these special occasions, the treehouse would appear as a secure place to watch.

When the treehouse was finally complete, the lift having been made last, Kerry formally invited her mother to the christening of the treehouse by having a tea party. Kerry could tell from the look of joy on her mother's face that she was going to make an announcement.

"So, this is what the pair of you have been creating over the last three months. It is wonderful, and the view of the yard means you will always know where we are in the garden." Suddenly, her face took on an absent look, and Kerry wondered if she too was seeing Celeste.

"This seems the appropriate time to let you both know that… I'm pregnant." The serenity on her face as she spoke, let Kerry know that she wanted this so badly.

Surprised, her father swept up the love of his life, placing the first kiss Kerry had seen him give her mother in a long time, on her lips. Over their heads, she could see Celeste, above their immediate eye level, smiling down on them all.

With the treehouse finished, Kerry planned some projects for herself and her father for the months ahead, including putting up a fence, down to the lake edge, with a locking gate. This time, her imagination conjured up the image of Aaron; she no longer needed to ask Celeste.

Judges' Comments: *An emotional and genuine story. I got invested in the outcome of the tree house; moved by the actions of a little girl to protect a brother who hadn't yet arrived. Enjoyed the story and was easy to read. Full marks.*

THE MONSTER UNDER THE BED

By Maureen Edwards

1st Runner-Up

Anna lay in bed, her muscles rigid, teeth clenched, eyes shut. 'I can't sleep in this place! Someone was smoking cigarettes all night, ugh,' she thought.

The two-bedroom apartment, in the noisy, congested city, was a stark difference from the serene, luxurious townhouse in the suburbs where she could stay hidden from everyone and everything. Still furious over her parents' separation after thirteen years, Anna had not spoken to her mother, Bella since they arrived.

A gentle knock on the door startled her, "Time for school. Let's go, honey."

Anna rolled her eyes. 'I swear her voice is like fingernails on a chalkboard,' she decided, as she put on her school uniform: blue jeans, Nike sneakers, a Taylor Swift concert t-shirt. Her room walls were bare; only pale pink splashes of paint since she refused to complete the task her mother had given her. 'Hardly enough room for my stuff in here.'

Slamming the bedroom door closed, she stomped into the bathroom, washed her face, and brushed her teeth.

The smell of Bella's strong perfume still invaded

the space. Anna avoided looking closely at the pristine white tile floors and cream marble walls. Instead, she focused on the window above the toilet. 'Huh, a perfect place to jump. Good to know.'

Being ready, she slowly moved into the kitchen, moping at finding her favorite breakfast, oatmeal with cinnamon, along with a white pill sat next to the bowl.

"Ready for a new day! I bet you it will be better than yesterday!" Bella, dressed in her baby blue nursing scrubs, stared at her cell phone giggling as she read her social media posts.

Anna could feel the painful tightness in her throat again. 'Argh, on the phone again. Always on the phone.'

Bella clapped, "Two minutes, honey. The bus will be here, so hurry up."

Anna buried her white pill in the leftover cereal before throwing it in the garbage. 'Ha! She didn't even notice what I did, again.'

Bella whispered in her ear, "You will eventually speak to me. I know it."

She kissed the top of Anna's head before Anna stomped to the door. Glancing out the window, gripping her backpack tightly, she waited in silence until she saw the school bus. She dreaded the bus honk, but it was better than staying in this prison.

Anna flew out of the door without a word.

Day after day, Anna sat on the last row of the bus alone. Her eyes were fixated outside, looking at the bodegas, police cars, apartment buildings, pedestrians.

'Gotta' get off this bus, way too crowded, no one shuts up.'

The bus jolted to a stop as it arrived at the school. Anna followed the overcrowded groups of students moving from all the buses, into the building; like a herd of cattle. Her heartbeat pounded as she reported to the principals' office as previously requested. The email said to see Ms. Kim first thing.

The tall, slender Korean American principal sat in the office, waving Anna into the room, and offering her a chair to sit. "Anna, we don't have a lot of time. Tell me about the lunch money from yesterday."

Anna shrugged her shoulders, looking down at the floor. 'Like you'll believe me anyway.'

"I warned them that if they did it again, they are in detention," she announced, shaking her head so much that her brunette bob haircut bounced. "They wouldn't admit to stealing it, but I'll keep an eye on them." Ms. Kim closed her eyes and sighed, "Come to me if you have anything to share. Some of the kids can be tough here, but I will handle them."

Anna cracked her knuckles. 'Yeah, right, that's what they all say. Next time, I have to pick a quieter kid to borrow from.'

"I can't help you unless you tell me what happened. My door is always open. The bell is going to ring, so you had better go to class." Ms. Kim drummed her fingers into the desk in apparent frustration.

Anna nodded and left. 'Leave me alone. I can fight my own battles.'

Ms. Kim typed up the incident, shaking her head and pinching her lips together.

Anna sauntered to her first-period class, managing to arrive with all the other kids. Her teacher, Mrs. Alvaro, said, "Anna, stay outside for a second."

When the last student had entered the room, the brown-skinned brunette who was wearing a tight brown wrap dress, closed the classroom door. "I just checked your essay last night. Did you work on it with someone?"

Anna shook her head. 'The work is way too easy for me.'

"It looks exactly like another student's work. Did you leave it somewhere? Let someone copy it?" Mrs. Alvaro leaned closer towards Anna.

Anna shook her head. 'I could have written it better myself, but I have nothing to prove to you.'

Mrs. Alvaro whispered, "I know the other student. He's a pretty good kid, so I'm surprised he would cheat, but you never know. Be careful where you do your work. I won't ask you to redo it this time."

Anna's face was flushed. 'Ha! It's so easy to get away with stuff here.'

"You know you can trust me. If you have something to tell, you can email me or just jot me a note." Ms. Alvaro patted Anna's shoulder and winked, "Go on in."

Anna's legs trembled as she walked into the classroom. 'This place is a joke. Much easier than my last school.' As she entered, Anna scanned the class in search of her next prey.

On the bus ride home, Anna found two older boys in her seat at the back of the bus. 'These guys have no idea who they are messing with.'

Mr. Joe, the bus driver who looked like a retired bouncer at a bar, heard cursing and screaming. Looking into the rear-view mirror, he shouted, "Hey, kid, come sit up here." He pointed to the front row seat with his middle finger. "We have to go. I have a schedule to keep."

Anna threw her bag on the empty seat, flopping down in a huff. Taking deep breaths, she bit her nails the entire ride. As Mr. Joe stopped at her apartment, he put his forearm up to block her from leaving the bus. She noticed his tattoo, which read, 'RIP MOM.'

"Hey, those boys bothering you? I can do something to end that real fast."

Anna scowled, kicking the torn mat on the floor. 'OK, Tough guy. I bet you cried when you got that tattoo. Had to hurt.'

"Say the word. I know these kids, and they can be real jerks. One call to their parents and they will be in huge trouble."

Anna's cold, hard eyes met Mr. Joe's sympathetic gaze. 'Whatever. I can take care of myself.' And she ran off the bus.

Approaching the apartment, she stopped abruptly at the top step, as she found Bella, her arms crossed, sitting and tapping her toes. Bella pointed to the cement next to her, "Take a seat. We need to talk. Now."

Anna sat down slowly and carefully. She wished something exciting would happen. 'I wish a car would crash into the tree so I can get away from her.'

"Do you have something to tell me?" Bella's voice snapped Anna out of her fantasy.

Anna's heart raced as she moved a little further away from Bella. 'What could you possibly want? You don't notice anything I do.'

"I'm home early for a reason. Ms. Kim called me. She is concerned. What happened?" Bella leaned in closer to look at Anna.

Anna sat still, all the while looking at her sneakers. 'Took you long enough.'

Bella ran her hand through her hair. "Talk to

me! You haven't said one thing to me since we got here. Ms. Kim told me what's going on. If the kids are doing something to you, then you have to speak up! Unless…"

Anna's body was tense. 'Duh, Mom.'

Bella stood up, blew out a deep breath, and opened the door. "Go to your room now. I don't even know what to say to you right now."

Anna bolted into the house, ran to her room, and jumped on her bed. Her head was buried under her pillow as she sobbed herself to sleep. Sometime later, a gentle knock startled her.

"You awake?" Bella walked in and sitting on Anna's bed. She tussled her daughter's hair. "Almost time for dinner. You must be hungry. Ms. Kim says you have not eaten lunch since you started school." Anna stared up at the ceiling, biting her lip. "Please, honey, do you have anything to say to me?"

For the first time in weeks, Anna muttered, "There… is a monster under the bed."

"A monster?" Bella's mouth fell open. "What are you talking about? Do you want me to look? Are you scared of something?"

Anna nodded. 'Finally!'

Bella slowly knelt on the carpet next to Anna's bed and lifted the bed skirt. She squinted. "I need a light."

Anna flipped up the light switch, her fingers trembling. 'Finally! You notice me.'

Bella called out, patted her hands on the carpet, "Come and kneel next to me."

Anna knelt down next to Bella. "Look! Nothing to be afraid of. Do you see? Weeks of not speaking for this." Bella held her daughters' face in her hands. "You worked so hard to speak in your old school, and I don't want you to regress." Bella sighed deeply. "A monster? Are you taking your medication, Anna?"

Anna looked down. 'Finally.'

Bella threw her hands in the air, moved from her knees to sitting on the floor, and placed her cell phone on the bed. "You know what to do, Anna. Come out when you're ready." Bella rubbed Anna's arms, kissed the top of her head, and said, "I love you, honey." Then gulping back a tear, Bella stood, rubbed Anna's back, and left the room, leaving the door ajar.

Anna's heart raced; her brain was scrambled. Slowly she lifted the bed skirt, pulled out the twelve-inch flat mirror that used to be on the wall in her old bedroom. She stared at her reflection. Sad moist blue eyes, pursed pale pink lips, bright red rosy cheeks, surrounded by ratty brown curly hair stared back at her. Her lips motioned the words, "I need help," but nothing came out.

Her hands shook as she picked up the cell phone, found the number, and called her therapist.

A teardrop slowly fell from her left eye, down her cheek onto the rug, then she heard the familiar, caring voice pick up.

She murmured, "Help!"

Judges' Comments: Captivating story and well written. Was very emotional and I was pulled in. Left wanting to read more. A very moving story and relatable.

WHATEVER HAPPENED TO TEDDY BEAR
By Amanda George

Joint 3rd Runner Up

"…and young Mr. Bear will be able to answer that, won't he?" asked Miss Wilson, the woodworking teacher.

A snigger went around the workshop.

Leaning over, Teddy Bear's workbench mate punched him.

"Ow!" complained Teddy."

"Welcome back, Teddy" grinned Miss. Wilson. "Care to share with everyone what you were daydreaming about this morning?"

Teddy blushed bright crimson. "Didn't hear what you said, sorry Miss. Wilson" he admitted.

"Fancy joining me for a lunchtime detention?"

Teddy shook his head and stared at the floor.

"In that case, you'll be able to tell us all how many   different types of joints there are then, won't you?"

Teddy shook his head again.

"Would someone who was listening, and paying attention, care to enlighten him please?" sighed Miss. Wilson.

Everyone's hands shot up.

"Go for it, Louise?"

"There are hundreds, but we'll only be learning about five or six of 'em while we are here at school," said Louise.

"Bullseye! Way to go, Louise!" smiled Miss. Wilson. Louise grinned widely, puffing out her chest with pride.

"Today, we'll be learning about the most common type of joint, the dovetail joint. Does anyone know how to create this joint, or is it new to all of you?" asked Miss. Wilson.

Thankfully the day got better for Teddy after that.

That was until he caught the bus home. He was so busy daydreaming that he missed his stop. Meaning, he was thrown off at the last bus stop. Teddy didn't even know where he was so couldn't text his dad to come and get him.

Finally, Teddy went to the nearest house and knocked on the door.

A man answered and grinned.

"Where am I please?" Teddy asked.

"You're at my house… come on inside so I can keep you safe" grinned the man.

"But I don't even know you, and my parents said not to go anywhere alone after school," said Teddy.

"I just want to keep you safe… you can call your family from in here," said the man, opening the door wider.

"Can I trust you?"

"Of course! I won't hurt you!"

Teddy nervously walked through the door.

"I only wanna phone my dad. To get him to come and pick me up," said Teddy.

"I'll take you home if you want?"

"No. I want my dad to come and get me."

"I said I'll take you home in a bit," said the man, locking the door.

"Please, let me go home?" pleaded Teddy. "I'm scared, and I just want to be home with my family!"

"Tell you what, how about you start doing your homework while I make us both a drink and something to eat; then I'll take you home," said the man.

"I want to go home… now," Teddy whimpered.

"You'll be able to go home soon, I just want to get to know you a bit first," the man said, brushing a stray strand of hair away from Teddy's cheek.

Teddy was too scared to plead anymore. 'Maybe if I just keep quiet and do what he says without complaint, he'll take me home soon?' he told himself.

"Come and sit here on the sofa, next to me," said the man, patting the seat next to where he was sitting.

"What if I don't want to?" asked Teddy.

"Then you won't be getting out of here as quickly as you want," shrugged the man. "Do you want a cuppa or anything?"

"No," said Teddy.

"How about some pop then?"

"No"

"How about a slice of chocolate cake?"

"No!"

"It's lovely and rich and sweet and gooey."

Teddy started drooling at the description of the cake.

"I won't tell your parents you've had it if you don't want me to," winked the man.

"I just want to go home, please," requested Teddy.

"I'll take you back when you've had a cuppa and slice of cake with me," promised the man. "I don't get a lot of visitors here so I wanna make the most of the opportunity."

After a few hours of being locked in the house, there was a knock at the front door.

The man cracked the door open a little bit.

"Yes?"

"Sorry to disturb you so late, but I was just wondering if you'd seen my son anywhere around here, please?" It was a voice that Teddy immediately recognised.

"Dad! I'm in here! Please take me home!" Teddy cried, running at top speed to the door and trying to squeeze past the man.

"We were just having a chat, a drink, and a slice of cake... want to join us?"

"I just want to take my son home, and it sounds as if he wants to leave too; so please let him out," demanded Dad. "Unless you want me to call the police?"

The man nodded, reluctantly stepping aside.

Teddy ran out, flinging himself at his dad in floods of tears.

"Let's get you home, Little Man... I've been so worried about you and why you didn't come home from school. None of your friends had seen you, so I phoned the school who contacted the bus company.

The driver said he had kicked you out just up the road from here, so I've been searching for you ever since," his Dad told him. "Why didn't you call me from your mobile?"

"It ran out of charge. Thank you so, so, much for rescuing me from that man, Dad!"

"I'll let the police know that you're safe… we were all wondering where our little Teddy Bear had got to and what had happened to him," winked Dad, with a chuckle.

And picking Teddy up, he placed him on his shoulders, and they set off home.

Judges' Comments: *This story drew me into its world. And there is a parallel with our world too! Very moving! I was drawn into the situation! A good ending. I enjoyed reading it! Teddy came to life!*

CLEO THE FRIENDLY CROCODILE

By Dorit Olive-Wolff

Joint 3rd Runner Up

As you can imagine, Cleo the Crocodile lived on the sandy shores of the river Nile. Cleo was a female crocodile. And as she grew up, all she could think about was having a baby crocodile all of her own. Cleo's sisters and cousins, even her friends, all had babies, sadly that is all except Cleo. This made her feel very, very, sad. Of course, Cleo was always willing to help whenever a babysitter was needed.

Every evening just as the sun was ready to disappear behind the Nile, Cleo would sigh, and pray to whomever crocodiles pray to. She would say: 'Please almighty benefactor of all the crocodiles, please let me have a baby crocodile of my own. I promise I will be good to my baby, and care for it.'

Many sunsets passed before one day, everything seemed different. Cleo felt different, and even her sisters commented on how different she looked.

"Well, Cleo," they would snigger. "Perhaps it comes from all those long swims you have after sunset."

And they kept on teasing her. Until, after many months, on one beautiful morning, Cleo laid an egg into the deep hole, which she had prepared on the sandy beach. Cleo never left the egg unprotected, not even for one single moment. Her sisters and friends had to bring her food as she would rather starve to death than leave her precious egg unprotected. She could hardly wait for the egg to hatch. And so, Cleo waited. But one cannot hurry such matters. Meaning Cleo had no choice but to patiently wait.

Finally, one day the egg started to move, and from inside the shell, Cleo could hear pick, pick, pick, pick. Bit by bit the baby crocodile picked its way at the egg until the opening was large enough for it to come out of the shell. The baby was so tiny and fragile, and at that very moment, there was no happier creature in the whole wide world than Cleo. You should have seen her smile! As she looked at her baby, she shed one big crocodile tear which fell straight onto the baby crocodile. The tear covered it all over, like a warm bath of loving-kindness. Being covered all over by Mummy Cleo's tear created a scent that would always be imprinted on the baby crocodile. It was this smell that would allow Cleo to always recognise her baby crocodile from any other. The scent of his Mother's teardrop.

Cleo was the most loving and caring of Mothers. She and her baby were always together, becoming completely inseparable. The little crocodile, being a boy, was named Cass. Cleo knew she would teach him all she knew, as well as what all crocodiles needed to know in order to survive, for

even crocodiles have enemies. There are some crocodiles who are hunted for their skins, which are used to make handbags, shoes, belts, and all sorts of other things.

There was danger from other animals, although there were not too many who dared to pick a fight with a crocodile, especially a fully grown crocodile. This meant the younger ones were in danger until they grew up and learnt all the pitfalls of life. Cleo knew that every day there were new things for her baby to learn. Learning stuff is endless. Whether it is a human baby or an animal baby, everyone has to learn how to grow up, and growing up is not easy at all. So, while being a Mummy is a very wonderful experience, it is also a very difficult one.

Cleo liked to sing to Cass before he went to sleep: "It's not so easy to be a Mummy. It's not so easy, believe me, child. To have an answer to all those questions, to all those ifs and buts and whys. It's not so easy, it's not so easy, it's not so easy, but it's very nice."

As Cass grew into a bigger boy crocodile, he began to be very curious and was full of the spirit of adventure. He wanted to explore the surroundings. But Cleo had warned him that he must never, ever go farther than being within earshot, so if he called out, she could come to his rescue. Cass was an obedient and loving son, and he and his Mother had a lot of fun together.

Cleo taught him how to hunt for food, how to avoid traps, and they often spent hours and hours basking in the sun.

Sometimes Cleo's sisters came to visit with their families. They would tell stories about the exciting and dangerous experiences they had all had. Each one of their stories was an important lesson because it was an example of how they had survived and were still able to tell the tale.

The youngsters listened carefully. They too had stories to tell, but most of them did not dare to as they knew they should not have got themselves into trouble. They also knew they should have obeyed their Mothers, especially after they were warned to keep away from fully grown male crocodiles. Cass listened with great interest, becoming more and more curious about the world beyond the Nile.

As siesta time approached, Cass took his usual place next to his Mother. But, as soon as Cleo was asleep, he quietly slithered away, following a small lizard he wanted to chase and play with. He didn't want to have a siesta, not today.

The lizard was very swift and agile. It crawled under a rock. Well, it was so much smaller than a crocodile. Cass was fascinated with his new little friend, but Cass also knew a few tricks himself. He could lie perfectly still without motion amongst leaves and trunks. This camouflage was so perfect that often other animals would step on him, thinking he was a part of the tree trunk, only to find out to their horror

that he was, in fact, a real crocodile. So, the two of them, Cass and the lizard, showed each other what they could do. It was fun.

The little lizard demonstrated his own unique trick. He could also lay totally still waiting for a fly, a grasshopper, or any small insect to settle. As they did, the lizard's tongue would shoot out with the speed of lightning and catch the insect, where it would disappear into his mouth and vanish. That was the best lizards' trick that Cass enjoyed.

He, of course, did not have such a tongue, which is why he asked the lizard to show him the trick again and again. And despite his best efforts, Cass could still not do it.

The sun was slowly disappearing from the firmament when Cleo woke up from her siesta. She was ready to dive into the water for the big evening meal. Looking around, Cass was not there. She called his name. First quietly, as she thought he might have gone for a little dip, maybe for a small snack before dinner. She knew he would not dare to hunt for a big meal on his own. Crocodiles usually hunted in pairs, and a young crocodile could easily become another larger crocodile's evening meal. She asked the other crocodiles if they had seen Cass. But no one had.

By this time, Cass was getting tired from running around. He was also feeling hungry. Getting food was always a special time for him and his mother.

Feeding time was always full of excitement. His Mother was an excellent hunter. She was quick and strong. No prey had ever escaped her. He knew he still had a lot to learn before he would have anywhere near the skill his mother possessed. Cass was very proud of his mother; she was a wonderful provider. He would never go hungry while growing up as he would always have his Mother to look after him. And when she became old and toothless, he would feed her, chewing her food for her. He would also protect her as she protected him now.

Suddenly he began to feel very lonely and worried, calling out for his mother, but there was no answer. He called again. This time a bit louder. Still no reply. Nothing.

He ran in all directions, but it seemed that he had wandered further away than he thought he had. Playing with the lizard, he had not noticed either the time or that he had wandered so far. He was worried he could not find his way back to his mother. Cass was becoming very frightened, and above all, he was sorry to have disobeyed his mother. She must be worried out of her skin.

Cleo too was calling out for Cass, but there was no answer. She was starting to feel heartbroken over what could have happened to her loving son? Had the hunters caught him? Had another crocodile eaten him for his dinner? Had he been in a fight? There were so many dangerous things that could happen, even to a crocodile, especially to a young inexperienced one.

Suddenly Cleo burst into tears. She cried real crocodile tears. She cried and cried. In fact, she couldn't stop crying. The tears just flowed. They poured out so much that they formed a stream which began to run over the savannas, under the rocks, bending left, then right. On and on they flowed. Cleo could not stop her tears; she cried a river full of tears.

Cass was tired, and he too was crying. He cried so much that he fell asleep, still sobbing. Slowly, Cleo's crocodile tears river began to flow past where Cass had gone one. The river of tears started to catch up with him. When he woke, he found himself surrounded by a pool of a very familiar scent. It was the scent imprinted on him the day he was born when his mother's first tear had dropped on him. The scent that would always be unique to him, and through this scent, his mother, and he would always be able to recognise each other.

All of a sudden Cass knew he was somewhere close to his mother. Following the river of tears, he knew his mother must have sent it to him so he could find his way back to her.

He followed it up the hills, and down the valleys, around rocks, and over the rocks. On it went. His small legs could hardly cope, but he struggled on. On and on he went until at last, he saw his mother crying, the tears pouring from her eyes.

He waved, but she did not see him as she was still crying. "Mother, Mother," he called.

"Son, where are you?" she cried back.

"Here I am," he sobbed.

"Where," she asked. "Where are you, Son?"

"I am here," he cried.

But Cleo could not see him. She had cried her eyes out. She had no more tears left in herself. She had used them all up in order to create the river which would bring the son she loved so much back, to her.

"Oh, mother," Cass cried. "I did not mean to cause you such pain. You loved me so much that you sacrificed your eyes for me. Mother, please forgive me. I will never leave you! I will look after you, I will protect you, provide for you, just like you have always cared for me."

By now, Cleo had stopped crying, and a smile had appeared on her face, a real crocodile smile. She was happy her son was safely home.

Cleo and Cass spent many more happy years together, being inseparable again. Only now the rules had changed for it was Cass who looked after Cleo. He fed her with the best food. He swam close beside her, protecting her from danger.

By now he was a fully grown crocodile. And Cleo and Cass became a legend among the animal kingdom. Even to this day, the story of the crocodile tears is told by parents to their children.

Judges' Comments: *Lovely introduction. I felt an immediate sympathy & connection with Cleo. It unfolds very well & I felt involved & anxious to see how it would end. The conclusion is cleverly drawn together, but the story would have a greater impact if the final sentence could be deleted.*
MW Note: *As this story is copyright to the author we have left the final sentence in. It is down to the readers to decide?*

THE MONSTER UNDER MY BED

By Willow Bowen

Our Youngest Entrant

BANG!

I woke up to a loud noise. Was I dreaming? I don't know. I pondered about hitting myself to see if I was awake or not.

Finally, I chose.

'Slap!'

"Ouch!" I screamed, immediately clapping my hand over my mouth. I forgot I was the only one awake.

After what seemed like an hour of waiting for another sound similar to the one which had woken me, I decided it probably wasn't going to happen again, so I could go back to sleep, which is what I did.

Suddenly, I was awake once again. There had been no noise this time to wake me. Maybe it had been the wind?

BANG!

There was that noise again; only this time, it was louder. And, it seemed as if it was coming from under my bed?

"Daddy!" I shouted. There was silence.

I shouted again; only this time louder, "**DADDY**!"

Should I go into my parent's room or should I stay put?

Whilst deciding what to do, the choice was taken away from me when, unexpectedly, the door slammed shut.

In all my life, I had never been as scared as I now was. The last time I been scared like this was last summer when I was sure I had seen something dash across my room. Back then, I had gathered up my braveness and gone to investigate. It turned out to be my cat, trying to get into my wardrobe.

I began to think that maybe I could do what I did last time. But the thought of what was lurking underneath my bed, making the banging noises overwhelmed me. I was frightened and dared not check under the bed. Gathering the blankets around me, I snuggled down into the bed, hardly daring to breathe, all the while wishing my daddy would come soon.

After a long time of trying to get back to sleep, I suddenly heard a soft thumping noise coming from somewhere near where the last bang had come from.

Peeking through a gap in the sheet, all I could see was darkness. Nothing but black, darkness.

That was until my lava lamp flickered on, and lit up the whole room. By this point, I was terrified.

Especially, as the thumping noise, was growing louder and louder.

Quickly, I hid back under my blanket, hoping and wishing that everything scary would fly away. But my wish was not to come true as the thumping grew louder and louder with every second.

Then there was silence. All at once, everything became deathly silent. What was I to do?

I tried to scream, but no sound left my mouth.

The last thing I remember was a slimy, clawed hand, as it reached from under my bed, slowly making its way towards my face...

Judges' Comments: *This was a delightful very short story. And one that could almost be true, not just created from imagination. The writer is quite young and we felt she had done very well for her first writing competition. We also felt that the story could actually be extended but we have left that to the writer to decide how she would like to progress it. Well done Willow for competing against the adults.*

A MAGICAL PAINTBRUSH

By Edith Robson

Jamie shoved his chair back and struggled past the rows of desks to the front of the class. He sighed as he reached the table - last to choose again.

One brush remained. Jamie's heart plummeted to his socks as he picked it up before returning to his seat. The other pupils were fiddling with brightly coloured new ones; blues, reds, yellows, and greens.

'What do I get?' he thought. 'A scabby looking thing, whose paint has peeled away, apart from one tiny smidgen at the end.'

"Who are you calling, scabby?" said a voice in his ear.

Jamie looked to the right and left. "Who said that?" he mumbled.

"I did, you great lummox. You should be thankful to have me at all. I am not just any old brush, you know."

Jamie's eyes nearly popped out of their sockets. 'A talking brush. Ahh come on, that's plain daft.'

"Are you saying I'm daft? I'll show you who's daft."

And a blast of blue paint hit Jamie in the face.

"Ow!"

"Is something the matter, Jamie?" Miss Jones looked up as her favourite scallywag, wiped paint from his face. He shook his head.

"Right then, everyone. Homework."

The class groaned.

"I would like you all to paint a card. If anyone doesn't have any paints, I can lend you some."

The questions bounced around the room... "What sort of card, Miss?" "When is it for, Miss?" "Can we trace a picture we like, Miss?"

Miss held up her hand for silence. "I thought we might make a cheer someone up card. Who likes surprises?"

A forest of hands shot up.

"There you are, then. I want to see a card that works magic. As if it is unexpected. It has to show the person you are thinking about them. It could be your Granny, or perhaps an Auntie who lives on their own. Bring it in on Monday, please."

* * * *

When Jamie got home, the voice asked, "So, what are we going to paint, then?"

"Dunno."

"Well, who is it for?"

"Mum, I suppose," muttered Jamie.

"Ok. What would Mum like?"

Jamie shrugged. "Flowers, maybe." He thought for a moment, then chose tulips.

"Great idea, man, simple shapes," said the voice.

Jamie thought, 'Praise from a magic paintbrush. Wow!'

"Draw them different heights. And have some drooping," said the paintbrush.

'Does he have to be so bossy?' Jamie wondered.

"My turn. I'll paint it," and all of a sudden, the brush leapt out of Jamie's hand and swiped across the bright green paint in the box.

It then started flashing back and forth, from paint to paper, all in a blur until finally, he announced, "Done!"

Then it swirled in the clean water and plopped itself down on the desk.

"Wow!" said Jamie.

The paintbrush said, "I am rather good, even if I say so myself."

"Only…"

"Only what?" asked the brush.

"Nothing. It's fine."

The next morning, Jamie stared at his desk.

"What did you do with it?" he shouted at the paintbrush, who was snoring away on the window ledge. The painting had vanished. All that work for nothing!

"Breakfast!" Mum called, as the doorbell rang.

He clattered downstairs, jumping on the third bottom step to make it shriek, which is what he wanted to do.

As he chewed the last spoonful of Fruitybix, Mum returned to the kitchen carrying a vase of beautiful, but odd-looking tulips. The stems were red, blue, and yellow, while the flowers were green.

"I don't know who sent these, but they are extraordinary."

Later, when they were on their own, Jamie stared at the paintbrush.

The paintbrush asked, "What?"

"Does everything you paint come to life?" asked Jamie.

"Yesss… but you have to be careful," said the brush slowly.

"What do you mean?"

"Well, for example, if you draw a mountain, this house and half the town would disappear under it."

Jamie's mind began to run with wild possibilities; like him having a Formula One racing car.

"You can't have one of those. It wouldn't fit into your bedroom for one thing. What about some sweets?" asked the brush.

That sounded good but drawing them wasn't as straightforward as Jamie had hoped. The results were a mixture of fruit, toffee, and chocolate. At least his pals would be happy. They ate all kinds of weird things.

"I need a new pair of trainers. But I don't think I can draw them," said Jamie.

"Do you want me to have a go?" But it turned out the paintbrush didn't understand what trainers were.

"I can't wear flip-flops for athletics," Jamie told him in exasperation.

"Well, make up your mind. This will be your last chance."

Jamie paced up and down, trying to decide what he wanted. Finally, he said, "I would really, really like a dog."

"Not if your Mum won't agree to one."

Jamie nodded, before visions of a curly scruff-ball faded from his hopes. "Could we make a kite then?"

"Sure, but can't you make one yourself?" asked the brush.

"Not with a dragon on it."

"Are you certain that's what you would like?" said the brush.

"Yes. Dad's too busy these days; and anyway, he can't draw either," announced Jamie.

Carefully Jamie drew the kite. Then he let the paintbrush draw the Dragon. Purple and green, with orangey-red flames spurting from its mouth, and a tail that stretched right across his bed. People would see it from miles away.

"That's super! Thank you," smiled Jamie.

It was later, in the middle of the night, that the smell of burning woke Jamie up. As he opened his eyes, he saw standing at the foot of his bed, a baby dragon, who was spouting flames.

"Stop," yelled Jamie, shocking the beast.

"Help! Help!" Flames were slowly working their way along the wood of the paintbrush.

Quickly, Jamie ran to the bathroom to hold the brush under the tap. Then, filling the toothmug with water, he threw the water over the dragon. Whoosh, it doused the flames.

"Quick, draw me another handle. I need to make the dragon disappear," said Jamie.

Placing the brush on a sheet of paper, Jamie drew round it and added a long wobbly handle. Within seconds, the brush looked as good as new. He waved his wet bristles in the air. Where the drops of water touched the dragon, it disappeared.

"I'm sorry," said the brush. "I should have warned you."

"My fault. I wanted a kite with a dragon on, so much."

Together, they cleaned up the bedroom. Tomorrow, Jamie would have to return the brush, but he still hadn't made the card for school. This time, he drew a puppy, colouring it in himself.

Next day, when he arrived home from school, Jamie found the kitchen floor covered in newspaper. All at once, he heard the sound of a yelp, and then paws pounding along the passageway. Kneeling, he was suddenly knocked over by a wiggly black body, with a long, lolling tongue, doing its best to lick his face.

"You'll need to help look after him," said his Mum.

Jamie grinning, declared he would, and his new best friend barked wildly as they both rolled across the floor.

__Judges' Comments:__ Very strong opening, throwing the reader straight into the action. Lots of "showing" rather than "telling" and some good use of the senses to draw the reader into the story. I really enjoyed this one.

THE FRIENDLY CROCODILE

By Joy Lynn

Charlie was a very friendly crocodile. He had just moved into No. 1 Chestnut Gardens, having spent the entire weekend unpacking all his boxes, and putting his furniture exactly where he wanted it.

When he woke up on Monday morning, he thought to himself, 'How lovely it will be if I can meet my neighbours and make some new friends.' So that evening, he knocked at the door of No. 2 to introduce himself. The door was opened by a big brown bear, who was wearing a dark blue suit and carrying a very large, black briefcase. The bear did not look particularly pleased to see Charlie.

"Hello," said Charlie, smiling at the bear. "I have just moved into No. 1, and I wondered if you would like to be friends?"

The bear stared at him, then he said, "I have just had a very busy day at work. I am too tired to make a new friend today," and he closed the door.

Charlie stood for a moment looking at the closed door, before walking back down the garden path. But as he left, he noticed how the bear's garden gate needed repairing as it was hanging off by the hinges.

'As Mr. Bear is so busy at work, perhaps I can repair the gate for him,' thought Charlie. So, he went and collected his toolkit and fixed the hinges on the gate, making it as good as new. On his way back home, he did not notice Mr. Bear watching him from behind his curtains.

On Tuesday morning, Charlie knocked at the door of No. 3. The door was opened by a very pale-looking pink flamingo who was sniffling and looking generally unwell. She was holding a pink spotted handkerchief to her rather red nose.

"Hello," said Charlie, "I have just moved into No. 1, and I wondered if you would like to be friends?"

The flamingo sneezed, then wiped her nose with her handkerchief. "I am feeling very poorly and am too ill to make a new friend today," she said and closed the door.

As he walked back down the path, Charlie thought, 'Perhaps Mrs. Flamingo will feel better if she has something nice to eat?'

So, he went to the corner shop and bought some bread, butter, milk, and cheese, leaving them on her doorstep. On his way back home, he did not notice Mrs. Flamingo watching him from behind her curtains.

On Wednesday morning Charlie knocked at the door of No 4. To his surprise, the letterbox flap lifted, and a pair of eyes looked out at him. "Hello," said Charlie "I have just moved into No 1, and I wondered if you would like to be friends?"

The door was opened, just a crack, by a small penguin, who went bright red when she saw him. "I am not good at talking to people," whispered the penguin, "and am too shy to make a new friend today," and she closed the door.

'Perhaps Miss. Penguin likes reading instead,' thought Charlie, so he went to the library, borrowed one of his favourite books, and left it on Miss. Penguin's doorstep. On his way back home, he did not notice Miss. Penguin watching him from behind her curtains.

On Thursday evening Charlie knocked at the door of No 5. There was a lot of noise coming from inside. The music (for that is what the noise was) stopped. Suddenly the door was opened by a monkey holding a trumpet.

"Hello," said Charlie. "I have just moved into No 1, and I wondered if you would like to be friends?"

"I am in the middle of my practice," said the monkey. "I don't have time to make a new friend today," and he closed the door.

'As Mr. Monkey is musical, perhaps he likes attending concerts,' thought Charlie. 'I know that the local brass band is playing at the town hall in two weeks.' So, Charlie went and bought a couple of tickets, leaving them on the monkey's doorstep. On his way back home, he did not notice Mr. Monkey watching him from behind his curtains.

On Friday morning Charlie knocked on the door of No 6. He could hear lots of crying inside. The door was opened by a lion, whose mane was standing on end as if it had not been combed for a while. It also had lots of cereal stuck in it. There was also milk trickling down the lion's face and off the end of his whiskers.

"Hello," said Charlie. "I have just moved into No 1, and I wondered if you would like to be friends?"

"I am trying to get my daughter to eat her breakfast," said the lion, "and am feeling too stressed to make a new friend today," and he closed the door.

'Even if Mr. Lion does not want a new friend, perhaps his daughter does,' thought Charlie. So, he went to the toy shop and bought a teddy bear which he left on Mr. Lion's doorstep. On his way back home, he did not notice Mr. Lion watching him from behind his curtains.

On Saturday morning, Charlie was feeling a bit lonely. He had tried to make new friends, but none of his neighbours had been interested. Suddenly, Charlie heard a knock at the door. When he opened it, he saw Mr. Bear, Mrs. Flamingo, Miss. Penguin, Mr. Monkey, and Mr. Lion.

"Hello," said the bear. "My name is Benjamin. Thank you for repairing my gate. I am sorry if I was rude. I had a bad day at work, but I have brought you a rose bush for your garden to apologise. We could plant it together this weekend."

"That would be lovely," said Charlie and gave Benjamin a big crocodile smile.

"Hello," said Mrs. Flamingo. "My name is Fiona. Thank you for buying me some food – I am feeling much better now. I have brought you some cookies and a chocolate cake. Would you like to pop round for tea on Sunday?"

"That would be very nice, thank you," said Charlie, and he gave Fiona a big crocodile smile.

"Hello," said Miss. Penguin. "My name is Paige. Thank you for the book - I am enjoying it. Perhaps we could start a Book Club together; for all the people in the neighbourhood? It might help me overcome my shyness."

"That would be brilliant," said Charlie and he gave Paige a big crocodile smile.

"Hello," said Mr. Monkey. "My name is Milo. I am sorry I did not invite you in last Thursday; I was trying to learn a particularly difficult piece of music. Thank you for the concert tickets. I wondered if you would like to come with me as it is much more fun than going alone."

"That would be great," said Charlie and he gave Milo a big crocodile smile.

"Hello," said Mr. Lion. "My name is Liam. Thank you for the teddy bear – my daughter loves it. When you knocked on my door yesterday morning, she had just thrown her bowl of cereal over me, so your timing was not great! It is my daughter's birthday party this afternoon, and I wondered if you would like to come so you can see for yourself that she is not usually so naughty."

"That would be fun," said Charlie, and he gave Liam a big crocodile smile.

"Why don't you all come inside," he said, "and we can have some tea and share these lovely cookies."

And so, Benjamin, Fiona, Paige, Milo, and Liam went inside and sat down at Charlie's kitchen table. Charlie put the kettle on to boil and looked around at all his new friends. 'How lucky I am,' he thought. 'It's a good job I am such a friendly crocodile.'

Judges' Comments: A jolly tale of how to build a friendship. I really liked this story. Lots of variety in the characters which help children to understand that no matter how diverse we people are we can still mix and get on. Well done.

THE SECRET LIFE OF A DINNER LADY

By Colin R Parsons

I'd suspected something for a while about Mrs. Travis, our dinner lady. She's by far my favourite out of all the ladies, but I wouldn't tell that to the others. Mrs. Travis tries not to stand out, but there is something different about her.

I asked my friends about her, but they just laughed and said I was an idiot.

"She's a dinner lady – deal with it," Brad said one day, "Unless you fancy her?" he continued with a grin. "You fancy her, don't you?" he teased.

"Shut up. I don't fancy Mrs. Travis." I grimaced, my cheeks reddening. "She's just nice to me," I snapped. And for a while after that, I didn't mention her to my friends because they would tease me.

It was a few weeks later when something happened. I was waiting in the dinner queue. It was a Wednesday. I remember that because it was Darryl's birthday and we were all invited to a party at McDonald's after school. On that day, I was about halfway along the line. From where I was standing, I could see directly behind the stainless-steel serving counter. No one else noticed in all the confusion of the lunchtime rush. You could barely hear anything above the commotion of screaming voices and jostling kids. I had my empty tray, which I was sliding along the rail, while the girl in front was getting served.

Then it happened!

Mrs. Travis was dishing out mashed potato with a scoop, which isn't really top news, but... she dropped a blob of potato on the floor, on her side of the counter. The part which is hidden from the others. It should have gone splat.

But it never landed... and that's what caught my attention.

As I looked, the potato fell within a few centimetres of the floor, stopped, then it just hung there! In mid-air. Mrs. Travis – without looking down, held out her ladle and the splodge of mashed potato lifted up and plopped back onto her scoop.

The other dinner ladies were far too busy to see what had happened. But I had seen it, and at that moment Mrs. Travis glanced over to me. Our eyes met, and I remember my mouth dropping open like a fish. Her steel-blue eyes were mesmerising as she held my gaze for what felt like minutes but must have been mere seconds. Then she finished serving the girl, and it was my turn to step forward. I was nervous, confused, still trying to work out in my head if what I had seen had actually happened, or not! I turned to face her.

"Would you like some potato with your chicken, Jamie?" she asked as if nothing had taken place. I opened my mouth to speak, but only a croak came out. "Are you okay?" she pressed, peering at me with those translucent eyes.

"Err, um yes, Miss. I'll have potato – yeah potato," I stumbled over the words. The children behind me were laughing at my expense, but I could barely hear them – I was so embarrassed.

At the end of that school day, I went to the party. When I got home, I was so tired I went straight to my bedroom, still pondering about the strange thing I'd seen. I ran the memory through my mind again and again – like movie footage.

But the more I recalled – the more muddied the memory became. Finally, in the end, I dismissed it all together and went to sleep.

It wasn't until a few weeks later that something else occurred. It was one Saturday morning, and I was in town with my friends Darryl and Brad. We were going to the video game shop as Darryl had a load of birthday money, and he wanted to buy the latest version of Deck Wars. Deck Wars is a cool game, but I've only got the older version on my console.

We were going our separate ways when Brad and Darryl noticed Mrs. Travis in the car park. They began teasing me again. "Why don't you ask her out, Jamie?" they taunted, nudging me in the back.

"Go on," Darryl said, "or she'll drive away, and you'll miss your chance forever."

"Shut up, you Muppets," I responded. "I'll see you on Monday," and slowly made my way in the opposite direction.

I could still hear them laughing in the distance as they disappeared behind the shops.

I don't know why, but I stopped at the end of the railings and watched as Mrs. Travis got into her car. She sat inside, and I could hear the engine trying to start, but for some reason, it wouldn't. I'd done some mechanical workshops at school and knew you had to have a good spark for the engine to start up. It then occurred to me that maybe I could help her, or not – I was too nervous to go over. But then, Mrs. Travis got out of her car and stood by the bonnet. She looked around the car park. Probably to see if anyone was watching her.

I instinctively dived down so as not to be seen, but then I thought, this is getting ridiculous. So, I got back up to see if I could help out. She didn't see me because she was concentrating with her eyes shut while having her right hand resting on the bonnet. I looked on curiously.

Suddenly, the car started up! In an instant! And… as she pulled her hand away from the metal surface, I swear I saw white bursts of electricity discharge from her fingertips.

She must have realised she was being watched as she looked up, I dropped straight down out of sight again. Did she see me? How on earth had she done that? Is she an alien? All those theories were swirling around in my head. What was I going to do? While all his was going on in my head, I heard a car door shut, then the sound of a vehicle pulling away.

Clambering back up to take a look was my mistake, for there was Mrs. Travis; standing right in front of the car I was hiding behind. I swallowed hard, feeling my body trembling.

"Hello, Jamie," she said with her soft, sweet voice. "Are you okay?" adding, "You look a little pale."

"I-I'm all right, Mrs. Travis, err honestly," I lied, my breathing laboured.

"Would you like a bottle of water?" she asked, giving me a warm smile and revealing two rows of

glowing-white teeth.

"I… I…" I stuttered.

"I've got one in the car, come on," and she gestured me to follow her.

I was in shock from the car engine thing, as well as in turmoil over what to do. Should I go to her car? It would be impolite to refuse; after all, she was our dinner lady. But a dinner lady who could stop mash potato from hitting the floor, and who could start a car engine with just a touch, well? I did the only thing I could - I panicked and ran.

I could hear her shouts of protest as I legged it down the high street. I ran for a while, stopping only to catch my breath. That's when I heard a car pull up alongside me. Turning, I saw Mrs. Travis sitting in the driver's seat. She rolled down the passenger window, but I wasn't listening and cut away to run across the grass to the park. I knew I could disappear in there. She wouldn't be able to follow me in her car. And there was a gate on the other side of the park which led to my estate.

It was a hot day, and I was already sweating from my sprint along the road. I could feel the sweat pouring down my cheeks from my forehead. Sweat stung my eyes, making my nose run. As I sped along the pathways, I rubbed the back of my bare arm across my leaking nostrils. Soon my lungs were burning, my legs feeling like concrete.

I took a glance over my shoulder to see if I was being followed, and that was my next biggest mistake! All of a sudden, I tripped over my own feet, stumbled off the path, and rolled down a grassy embankment. As I tumbled down the freshly cut slope, blades of grass cuttings flew up in my face, filling my open mouth. Eventually, I came to a stop at the bottom, landing on my back.

The world was spinning as I gasped for air. Choking, I spat out strands of damp grass. I could hear my heart thudding inside my head. My lungs struggled for oxygen. As the initial confusion began to subside, a headache boomed in my temples, forcing me to roll over on my side so I could throw up. I was a mess. Eventually, I sat up and opened my eyes.

I could feel the heat on my cheeks, my forehead pounding. The whole world appeared to be spinning.

My body ached from top to toe. And I needed a paper tissue to clean myself up but had to wait for things to settle. Reaching into my pockets, I realised both were empty. No tissue, phone, or my cash. When I looked around, I saw all the contents of my pockets scattered on the grass verge. I scoured further along, and to my utter dismay, saw Mrs. Travis staring down at me.

"Jamie. Are you all right?" she called.

Slowly, I wiped as much as I could of the vomit from my face with my hand and rubbed it off on the ground. Mrs. Travis was making her way down the embankment, stopping here and there to pick up my belongings. As she approached me, she pulled a small pack of wet wipes from her bag. Peeling the top back, she handed me a moist cloth. I cleaned away all the sweat, and remaining mess from my face, before taking another tissue to finish off.

Leaning forward, she handed me all the things that had fallen out of my pockets. "You're looking a bit hot, Jamie," she said with concern. Dipping back inside her bag, she fished out a bottle of water.

"Here, drink this," she insisted, handing me the plastic container. I swallowed hard – my throat dry from the hot temperature. "Do you live far from here?" she asked.

"I live just over there," I said, pointing to the estate beyond the fence of the park boundary.

"Come on; I'll walk you to your house," she said, giving me that amazing smile of hers. "Let me help you up," and with that, she gripped my arm and pulled me to my feet.

Strangely, as soon as I felt her touch, the warmth from her fingertips oozed energy into my body, and I felt a lot better. My headache was gone - I felt amazing.

"Is your mum home?"

"Yes," I answered, as we walked up the banking to the footpath. She chatted endlessly as we strolled to my street, and eventually to my door. Mrs. Travis insisted on knocking, and my mum came to answer.

"Jamie. Are you ok?" asked my mum looking straight past me to Mrs. Travis.

"He took a bit of a tumble in the park, Mrs. Morgan," she told my mum, "but I think he's all right." Mum was concerned, thanking Mrs. Travis profusely for looking after me.

I went to bed that night and slept well, waking the next morning with a weird feeling inside. I went to school as usual, and at mid-day, the bell sounded for lunch. I was in the dinner queue, thinking about Darryl's birthday. We were going to McDonald's after school for his party. I waited as Mrs. Travis was serving a girl in front of me.

Suddenly she dropped a blob of mashed potato. She sighed when it splatted on the floor; then she stooped down to pick it up. As she did, she looked over and gave me a wink!

Judges' Comments: *A lovely mixture of fantasy and reality. I enjoyed the story and could see this progressing into a longer series of adventures. Quirky tale. Well done.*

THE MYSTICAL TREE HOUSE

By Sebastian Stumblebum

"I'll be ten years old tomorrow; I'll be ten years old tomorrow," sang Jon, for what seemed like the hundredth time that morning.

"I know you're excited that it's going to be your birthday, but can you please stop saying it all the time?" pleaded his mother.

"Sorry Mum," said Jon sheepishly, "but it's finally my turn to visit the treehouse to choose my present. I am just so happy; I can't help it."

Jon, his family, and several dozen other families of all nationalities were living in an extraordinary part of South America. All were descendants of the adventurers and explorers, who had once travelled the world. And who had somehow discovered this spectacular valley hidden deep within the jungle? It was such a beautiful and magical place that not one single person who came upon it ever wanted to leave.

Over time, the valley became the home to a small group of like-minded people, who decided they would live nowhere else. At first, it was challenging to get the supplies needed to live. They had to travel for many days to the nearest town to buy food and clothing. To add to this problem, they were all trying to buy what was needed, in many different kinds of currency. The French tried to use Francs, the Spanish Pesos, the Japanese Yen, and so on.

Eventually, after one long and arduous journey, someone suggested that perhaps there was no need to travel anywhere. And maybe, they wouldn't need money of any kind. All they needed was each other. And to achieve this they would all band together.

Some families would be responsible for growing one particular type of vegetable. Others would plant fruit trees. At the same time, others would tend the cows, sheep, or goats. Even their clothing would be made in the village, using cloth woven from the sheep's wool, or from the cotton they could grow. Everyone would help provide the needs for everyone else.

The people thought the idea was marvellous and so a new community was formed. One in which everyone relied on each other for everything they needed to live. It was into this community that Jon had been born and would grow up.

There were also other surprising, exciting things, about this fascinating valley which can only be described, as magical. You see the valley was also home to a tribe of pixies. Although they lived at the very end of the valley, they too were prepared to help anyone, if it was needed. It was these wonderful beings who had shared the secret of the mystical treehouse.

About half an hour's walk from the centre of the village, perched on top of a small hill, was the most significant and strangest looking tree you could ever imagine. Although there was said to be a treehouse there, no sign of a house being built anywhere in its branches was visible. That was part of its exceptional secret. You see, the house was inside the tree.

The tree was covered in thick, green ivy and had massive gnarled roots which encircled the entire tree as if protecting it. They were there to hide another secret, the door. It was on this door that Jon would have to knock if he was to receive his birthday gift.

There aren't many celebrations among the village families as there are in the rest of the world, mainly because everyone who lived here was happy all the time. They didn't need to be told when to celebrate; life was always enjoyable.

However, there was one day, your birthday, which was always special. From the time you were able to walk to the tree on your own until you became an adult, the tree would provide you with a gift of your choice. Although it was indeed a mystical treehouse, to the children it was known as the birthday tree.

Deep inside the treehouse, were many rooms, all of different sizes, shapes, and colours. In some of these rooms, the pixies worked, making toys for the children's birthdays. It was something they loved doing, as they believed there was nothing better than seeing the smile on a child's face when they received a present.

For several months now, Jon had been wondering what he would like to have as his special present. Finally, he had decided on a fishing rod. At last, he would be able to go with his father on his weekly trips to the river, to catch the huge catfish which all the villagers enjoyed.

The long-awaited morning of his birthday finally arrived, and as it was also the tenth birthday of Lindsey, the little girl who lived just a few doors away. His mother had suggested they should go together.

Six months earlier, Lindsey had told Jon how she had already decided what she wanted for her birthday gift. "I have always wanted a beautiful china doll. One with long golden curls just like mine. With a doll, I will be able to pretend that I have a sister, and talk to her before I go to sleep at night. As you know, I only have brothers, and sometimes it would be nice to have a girl in the family to talk to, even if she isn't real."

Even though he was a young boy, Jon still understood what she meant, thinking that it was a good choice of present.

On the morning of their birthday, Jon went to Lindsey's home. Knocking several times on her door, he started to become slightly impatient, as he was anxious to start the short walk to the treehouse.

However, it wasn't Lindsey who answered the door, but her father. He told Jon that Lindsey was ill with a severe cold. It had come on overnight, and as it was a chilly and slightly damp morning, he could not risk her going outside. "It could make her cold worse.

I am afraid she will have to wait another year, until her next birthday before she visits the tree," he explained.

"I cannot imagine how disappointed she is," said Jon. "Please tell her that I hope she feels better soon," and with that, he left to make his way up the hill towards the mystical treehouse.

As he went along, Jon realised he was running with excitement. When he reached the top of the hill, he suddenly stopped, becoming nervous for finally, stood there before him, was the spectacular tree. Pausing for a couple of minutes to calm his breathing, he slowly approached the barely visible door nestled below one of the enormous roots.

The door was only slightly taller than him, and in the centre was a notice with the words, 'Welcome my young friends, knock twice, and I will open.'

Following the instructions, Jon knocked twice without delay, and was pleased to be greeted by one of the pixies, whose name he knew was Tiffany; although all her friends called her Tiff.

As he followed the pixie, Jon was led down a long staircase, to a room which he believed was at least twenty feet underground. He mentioned to Tiff that it all looked different from when he was last here for his ninth birthday.

"That is because every room is different for each year," explained the Pixie guide. "Now you are ten, your choice of gifts is unlike those you would have seen last year."

Looking around, Jon saw how the room was bathed in a hazy, silvery-blue light, meaning it was impossible to tell where the walls ended, or even if there were any walls at all.

This all added to the feeling of magic and awe that the visitors felt.

Jon was surrounded by tables of toys, and other astonishing, unusual gifts, such as balls that would only bounce sideways, and YoYo's which worked without string.

However, knowing what he wanted, Jon was led to a table displaying some of the most magnificent fishing rods he had ever seen. Including one, just like his father had received, when he was ten years old.

Even though the pixies had made all of these wonderful gifts, they still somehow always knew what the heart's desire of every young child in the valley was. Tiff pointed out the rod she thought he would like the best. For several minutes Jon looked at what he had been dreaming of for the past year, picking up one rod, then another, before carefully placing them back on the table.

Then unexpectedly, he turned around and walked towards a table at the far end of the room. One where he would find what he wanted, although he wasn't quite sure.

Finally, without any hesitation at all, he picked up what he knew would be the perfect birthday present. Turning towards Tiff, he said, "I would like this one, please."

The pixie smiled broadly. "I think that you have made an excellent choice," she said, and having placed his selection in a box, she escorted him to the exit door of the tree.

Arriving back in the village, Jon, instead of going directly to his home, stopped at the house of his friend Lindsey. Politely asking if he was able to see her for just a few minutes, her mother said that was fine, but not for long as she needed to rest.

Lindsey was surprised but pleased to see Jon, asking him what he had chosen as his birthday gift. Carefully Jon opened the box and taking out a beautiful china doll he gave it to his friend.

"Happy birthday, Lindsey," he said. "I can always go fishing with my dad, and take turns with his rod until next year. You need your doll more than I need a fishing rod."

For the first time in her young life, Lindsey was speechless. All she could do was hug her friend through tears of happiness.

Blushing a little, Jon mumbled that he did not want to risk catching her cold, so he should leave. "I will see you in a few days when you are feeling better. For now, you can cuddle up to your new sister," and he laughed, before going home.

His parents were not surprised when he told them what he had done. Everyone in the village knew Jon as a kind and loving child. Exhausted after a long day, Jon went to bed early, thinking about what the doll meant to Lindsey. He fell asleep with a smile on his face.

Early the next morning there was a brief knock on the door. When his mother went to answer it, she saw a pixie walking away. A box with Jon's name on had been left on the doorstep.

Waking up her son, she presented him with the box. It contained the best fishing rod he could ever have wished for. With it was a note.

'Any child who shows such unselfish behaviour, as you did yesterday, by forfeiting their heart's desire, deserves to be rewarded. Please accept this gift from all your new friends at the mystical treehouse. We look forward to seeing you on your next birthday visit. Signed, Tiff and friends.'

Jon was both surprised and delighted, insisting that he and his father go fishing immediately after breakfast, which of course his Dad agreed to do.

A short time later, they were sitting on the banks of the river casting their lines into the deep pool where the biggest fish were swimming. His father looked proudly at his son, thinking about how it is always a good thing to be kind.

Although you may not expect it, kindness always brings its rewards in some way, and the knowledgeable pixies once again had proved that to be true.

Judges' Comments: *This is a sweet story of kindness. The author does a lot of world-building in the opening paragraphs and you get a clear sense of the environment the characters live in. I did feel it was a bit preachy in parts but overall, a really nice tale.*

VISITING WONDERLAND

By Maureen Edwards

Rinsing his face off in the sink, blotting it dry with toilet paper from the stall, Eric Garcia was out of breath. He had three minutes to spare before the scheduled departure. Disappointed, Eric could not take a shower before school, so the sink would have to do. Smelling under his armpits, then his shirt, he was confident the cologne sample from the mall would cover the stench of urine on his clothes. A great trick he had learnt in middle school.

With one last look in the mirror, Eric checked his teeth, making sure there was no evidence of food from dinner the previous night. His brown curly hair had been too long yesterday, so the art class scissors were an answer to his prayer as he tidied up the top and sides.

Grabbing the new designer backpack, he had found at the start of the school year, he dusted off the dirt from the base, caused when he had misplaced it the one time he had taken the subway.

Eric pressed down on the wrinkles of his ill-fitting brown khaki pants. His burgundy loafers were so tight it pained him to walk. Then he pushed his shoulders back and hustled out of the bathroom. He nearly ran down the clean, marble hallways, then out through the twelve-foot metal doors from the prestigious high school, the eighth one he had attended in as many years.

As Eric approached the purple school van, he heard the melodic voice of his favourite teacher, Dr. Simone Franks.

"Eric, perfect timing as usual. Go on in and get a seat!" Her smile lit up his heart. Thirty years as a teacher, her skin was as pale as her grey bob haircut. She was dressed in her typical uniform of a black A-line dress, with a matching sweater. Red glasses hung around her neck on a red string.

Dr. Franks had two prosthetic legs below her knees, which never deterred her from doing anything. After losing her family in a car accident, many years back, her mission in life was now her students. If anyone asked, this was her favourite day of the year!

Stepping up into the van, Eric gulped, as the only seat vacant was next to his dreaded nemesis, Olivia Hunter. He only had her to beat for the top spot in the class. She was a stunning long-haired brunette with sparkling brown eyes, who wore her typical dirty black flats. She smiled warmly at Eric, moving over to make room for him. "You excited for today?"

Eric kept his eyes straight ahead. "Sure. I've never been there before."

Dr. Franks sat in the driver's seat for the forty-five-minute drive. The eight students, except for Eric, had headphones on in the silence. He, on the other hand, wanted to see and hear everything without distraction. He had only been in the city once in his life. Yet he had researched all he could before this trip. He was in awe of the packed streets, the speeding cars, double-sized buses, and the roar coming from the construction sites. His mouth was open, his eyes bulging.

Olivia's hand brushed his arm. "This place is amazing. Have you been here before?"

Eric's heart fluttered a little. "Never. It's more stunning than I imagined."

Olivia leaned over near his ear, "I'm a bit of a wreck today, have to admit it."

Eric rolled his eyes. "You will do an amazing job. I'm sure, but I will do better!"

They laughed in unison as Dr. Franks called out, "We are here, guys! Ivy League University!" The students roared with cheers, hoots, and hollers. Eric's hands were trembling so much he could barely clap. He fixated on the size of the majestic buildings of the campus. Olivia was looking out her window, blinking quickly, rubbing her sweaty hands on her ill-fitting dress, goosebumps running up her arms.

Dr. Franks reviewed the agenda for the two-hour visit. "Guys, you have all the information for your interviews. You will all amaze them, I am sure. You are all too humble, so brag about yourself and show off!" She clapped like a cheerleader. "You are all highly accomplished and deserve these spots. Any questions?" The van was silent. "Go for it. I will be here at the van when you are finished."

The students disembarked in silence. Eric took a deep breath, finding himself walking next to Olivia.

She always smelled like fresh coconut. "Is this what you want more than anything? This school?"

She blushed. "That's why I have worked so hard all these years."

Eric popped a mint into his mouth. He handed one to her too, saying, "Me too. You will do great."

As they walked in the front door of the large, red-brick building, he held the door for her. "Good luck. See you back at the van."

Olivia touched his arm and bit her lip. "Good luck to you too." Olivia headed right as Eric went left.

Two hours later, Dr. Franks stood at the van. She had had the most hysterical lunch with the Dean of Admissions, her college roommate, who always shared some confidential information about the few, precious acceptances. Dr. Franks was promised a text of any updates, as in the past, sometimes within an hour. Looking up, she saw Eric, Olivia, and the six other students approach the van together. "So how did it go, everyone?"

The students took the same seats for the ride home. She heard a roar of comments from them saying, "Terrific." "Killed-it." "Rocked." She tried to listen to see if Eric and Olivia had anything to say, but they were silent. Turning around, she noticed they were talking about something in hushed tones, almost secretly.

Dr. Frank's eyebrows turned down, "Guys, settle down a little. We are going to hit a lot of traffic going back so I will drop you off at your homes. Just let me know where to go when we get to town."

It took nearly three hours to arrive back in town. Dr. Franks stopped as the students each called out their addresses.

Finally, only Eric and Olivia remained. "So, where do you want me to drop you off?" Eric and Olivia gulped and took a deep breath.

"Eric? Olivia? Where is it going to be?" She saw them exchange glances at each other through the rear-view mirror.

Eric said, "You can drop me off at the McDonalds on Main Street. I can get home from there."

Olivia chimed in, "Me too, Dr. Franks."

She was thrilled to see Eric and Olivia becoming friendly. She was worried the competition for the top spot in the class would have alienated them. When she stopped the van, Dr. Franks read her text. "Oh. My. Goodness." She turned toward the backseat. "I am glad I have you both alone. I have some fantastic news to share, off the record, of course. You are both going to get offered a spot for the upcoming class! Congratulations!"

Olivia and Eric clapped and cheered; they even high-fived each other. Their cheeks were purple, with Olivia close to tears.

Dr. Franks put her finger up to her mouth, "Keep it under your hat for a little while, please!"

Olivia rubbed her hands, staring at Eric. "I can't believe we both got full scholarships, Eric! Both of us."

Dr. Franks' smile faded. " Err… Olivia, not full scholarships. Acceptances. They did not talk about full scholarships. If that were the case, I would have said that."

Eric looked down, squeezing his leg. Olivia's eyes welled up as she bit her lip.

Dr. Franks' heart raced. "I am sure there will be money for you to go, but not full scholarships."

Eric sighed, "Thank you, Dr. Franks, for everything. Today was the best day ever. No one has ever given me this kind of opportunity." He slid the door of the van open, hopped out, and with his head down, he walked away.

Olivia sniffed, blotting her eyes with a dirty tissue. "Dr. Franks. I could not agree more. You set up such a once-in-a-lifetime day for us, a dream come true!"

Her lip quivering, eyes blinking rapidly, Olivia too jumped out, shut the door, and followed Eric into the darkness.

Dr. Franks banged her hands on the steering wheel. She squinted her eyes as she watched Eric and Olivia change directions at the corner, before walking away from the residential section of town.

Slowly, Dr. Franks followed them in the van, keeping her distance. She pulled over, turned the van lights off, and watched as Eric and Olivia walked into a tall building that resembled a church. Grabbing her phone, she looked up the address of the building. It read: St. Dominic's Center: Shelter for At-Risk Youth.

Furiously, she called her former roommate's number, "Hey, listen. I need some help with my two kids. They need money! Tell me there is something you can do, some strings you can pull? I have never asked, ever! But they are too good not to go." Dr. Franks cursed under her breath. "I know, but I had to try."

Ending the call, she threw her cell into her bag. She stared at the building housing the two most gifted students she had ever taught, saying, "I'm so sorry, guys. So much for visiting wonderland."

Judges' Comments: Some good description throughout. The story was interesting & drew me into its world. I read it twice. I wanted to find out what happened & to some extent, I cared about the outcome. The plot was good. I enjoyed reading it.

A MAGICAL PAINTBRUSH

By Sebastian Stumblebum

Charlie was a girl who loved to read anything put in front of her. It could be a book, comic, or magazine. She would consume every single word it contained. Often including the silly advertisements, which were thrust in front of her.

One cold and rainy day, when Charlie had to stay indoors, she decided to read one of her favourite magazines about nature's strange and unusual animals. However, today, instead of being engrossed in the beautiful pictures, and information, her eyes were drawn to something else. Down in the bottom left corner of the first page was an advertisement which started with the word – 'free.'

Strangely, it did not say what was 'free,' but instead promised the best and most magical present any child could ever hope to receive. If she were able to solve the five riddles in the advertisement, then the prize would be hers. However, there was only one prize to be won, which meant the first person to send in the correct answers would become the winner.

It also said it would take a very exceptional kind of person to figure out the answers. Someone who had an understanding of how some things in life are relatively simple, and that there was no reason to look for complicated answers.

Here were the five riddles.

1. What question can you never answer yes to?

2. If you threw a white stone into the Red Sea, what would it become?

3. What is as big as an elephant, but weighs nothing at all?

4. What can you break, even if you never touch it or pick it up?

5. A school teacher, a plumber, and a hat maker were walking down the road together. Which one has the biggest hat?

For the rest of the afternoon, Charlie struggled to solve the riddles, thinking of all the complicated answers possible. Suddenly, she realised what was meant by looking for simple answers. It was only then that she was able to solve the riddles, doing so within minutes.

"Mummy, Mummy," she shouted. "I've solved all the riddles. I need to write them down and post them today so that I can win the special prize."

Her mother was so impressed, that as soon as her daughter had written out the answers, making sure her name and address were on the paper, she hurriedly made her way to the post office, ensuring the letter was there in time for the last collection of the day.

The following week seemed to be longer than usual, as it always is when you are anxiously waiting for something to happen.

Every day   Charlie would watch for the postman to arrive, hoping he would have a letter or parcel for her.

Finally, after almost two weeks since sending her letter, a package arrived with her name on it.

A small box about nine inches long and two inches wide arrived, and next to her name and address was written, 'Congratulations, you have won.'

Charlie's hands shook slightly as she quickly ripped the lid off the box, but seeing what it contained her excitement turned to confusion. Nestled on an old and stained piece of paper was an artist's paintbrush, and not even a new one. It was old and well used, with a few speckles of paint still showing on the wooden part. Even some of the bristles were missing.

Her disappointment soon turned to disgust, and then anger. She was supposed to get the best gift anyone could ever receive. Picking up the brush, Charlie threw it across the bedroom, where it landed on the small rug next to her bed.

"It's just a dirty old paintbrush," she cried to her mother as she left her room. "What can be so special about that?"

"I really can't answer that," her mother replied. "You sit down, and I will fetch a glass of milk, then maybe we can figure out between us why it is supposed to be so special."

Moments later, Charlie heard her mother call her name, only now her mother sounded angry.

"What have you done? Why is there red paint on your rug next to the brush? You didn't tell me you had used it. I will have to put it in the washing machine tomorrow and hope that the paint stain will come out."

"But I haven't used it. Honestly, I just threw it over there," Charlie answered.

Charlie became quiet, even feeling a little sad, and as soon as dinner was over, she went to her room. She ignored the brush which her mother had cleaned and placed on her dressing table. Charlie was upset at the way her day had turned out, so did what she loved doing the most.

She read one of her favourite books until finally, she fell asleep.

Early the next morning, as she stepped out of bed, Charlie was surprised once again. The red stain on her rug was no longer visible. The rug looked as good as new. She called out to her mother, "Did you wash my rug last night while I was asleep?"

"No, of course, I didn't. I am going to do it after we've had breakfast," her mother answered.

"Well," Charlie slowly began, "There is no longer any need for you to do that as the red mark has somehow disappeared – it's completely gone."

Turning her attention to the paintbrush on the dresser, she noticed a tiny amount of paint on the tip of the bristles, only it was no longer red. It was now a beautiful shade of blue. For the second time within twenty-four hours, Charlie was bewildered.

Entering her daughter's room, it was her mother's turn to be confused when Charlie pointed to the brush. It now had a small amount of yellow flowing from it.

"I think you had better take a look in the box the brush came in, there may be something in there which will explain why this is happening," suggested her mother.

Looking, Charlie muttered, "There was an old piece of paper in the bottom of the box, but I was too angry to want to look at it."

Retrieving the box from under the bed, where yesterday she had kicked it in a temper, she took out what appeared to be a stained, ancient-looking sheet of paper.

On it was written, 'This paintbrush is for a remarkable person. One who I hope will put it to good use the way I did when I was a child.'

Underneath the message was a rhyme that did indeed explain everything.

When first you cast your eyes on me
You may not like what you will see
I am old and worn, my bristles are few
But I am special, though only for you

So, hold me tight, believe in me
I am unique you soon will see

All your emotions I will impart
Whatever you feel within your heart

Paint all you want throughout the day
For when night comes it fades away
Then with the dawn, you can paint anew
And let your feelings come flowing through

So, use me well to beautify
And paint big rainbows in the sky
This gift is yours to forever share
All you must do is show you care.

A gift for that special child from the Wizard

Grumble the Great

"Mummy, do you remember that book you gave me last year? The one which had all those beautiful different colours in it, that explained how every colour and shade had a meaning of some kind. Red could mean angry or upset, Blue was calming, and Yellow was happy. The brush must paint everything I am feeling."

"Last night I was angry, so some red paint dripped out of it. This morning, because I was quiet and calm, it became blue, and then yellow because I am happy. Any emotion I have, it paints."

While Charlie held tightly on to what was now her best, ever, present, her mother picked up the old piece of paper to read it for herself. She wondered who this Wizard was that would give such a wonderful and magical gift to someone he didn't now.

Although she thought, maybe in a way he did know her daughter, even if he had never met her.

His advertisement said that it was for someone who could solve riddles and that they would have to be very special to do so, and her Charlie was most definitely a remarkable young lady.

Now that Charlie understood how the magic of the brush worked and knowing that whatever she painted would disappear overnight, meant Charlie could begin to paint in earnest. For the rest of the day, Charlie painted butterflies, and flowers, on the outside walls of her house. Then she painted on the garden fence.

"Every day I will be able to paint something new and beautiful for all our neighbours and friends to see," she told her mother. "Everyone will be able to share this wonderful gift."

Charlie even discovered that by imagining all seven colours of the rainbow and sweeping a big arc in the air, a perfect rainbow would suddenly appear above her in the sky.

Her mother meanwhile remembered the riddles and the answers that her daughter had scribbled on a notepad, laughing as she read them.

The Wizard was right; the answers were merely obvious. It just took a certain kind of mind to realise it.

This is what she read:

What question can you never answer yes to?

Answer. Are you asleep yet?

If you threw a white stone into the Red Sea, what would it become?

Answer. Wet.

What is as big as an elephant, but weighs nothing at all?

Answer. The elephant's shadow.

What can you break, even if you never touch it or pick it up?

Answer. Silence.

A school teacher, a plumber, and a hat maker were walking down the road together. Which one has the biggest hat?

Answer. The one with the biggest head.

"I have to agree with this amazing Wizard, my daughter is indeed very special, and now she has been given the best present anyone could ever give her; a magical paintbrush."

And Charlie's mother smiled warmly.

Judges' Comments: *It was easy to read. Very amusing, and I enjoyed reading it. I was drawn into its magical world of colour, but unfortunately, I think the end was a little too predictable. There was a lack of surprise which slightly weakened the impact of the story. Other than that well written.*

Made in the USA
Middletown, DE
07 September 2023

38145864R00056